Cow Jokes
125+ Funny Cow Jokes for Kids

Johnny B. Laughing

ISBN-13: 978-1534615908
ISBN-10: 1534615903

DEDICATION

This book is dedicated to everyone that loves a funny joke.
Laughter is one of the best gifts you can give. It always puts a smile
on your face, warms your heart, and makes you feel great.

CONTENTS

FUNNY COW JOKES

Q: What does a cow make when the sun comes out?

A: A shadow.

Q: What do you get when a cow goes to the beach with tanning oil?

A: Pre-tanned leather.

Q: What do you get if you cross a cow with an octopus?

A: A cow that can milk itself!

Q: Why do cows like being told jokes?

A: Because they like being amooooosed!

Q: What's the best way to make a bull sweat?

A: Put him in a tight jumper!

Q: If you had fifteen cows and five goats what would you have?

A: Plenty of milk!

Q: What is a cow's favorite TV show?

A: Dr. Moo!

Q: Why wouldn't anyone play with the little longhorn?

A: He was too much of a bully!

Q: Why was the calf afraid?

A: He was a cow-herd!

Q: Why was the woman arrested on a cattle ranch for wearing a silk dress?

A: She was charged with rustling!

Q: Why don't cows ever have any money?

A: Because the farmers milk them dry!

Q: Why doesn't Sweden export its cattle?

A: It wants to keep its Stockholm!

Q: Why do cows think cooks are mean?

A: They whip cream!

Q: Why did the moron give the sleepy cow a hammer?

A: He wanted her to hit the hay!

Q: Why did the farmer put his cow on the scales?

A: He wanted to see how much the milky weighed!

Q: Why did the farmer put brandy in the cow's food?

A: He wanted to raise stewed beef!

Q: Why did the farmer fence in the bull?

A: The farmer had too much of a steak in him to let him go!

Q: Why did the farmer feed money to his cow?

A: He wanted rich milk!

Q: Why did the cow jump over the moon?

A: To get to the Milky Way!

Q: Why did Bossy slug Roy Rogers?

A: She heard he was a cowpuncher!

Q: Why did Bossy tell the cowpoke to leave her calf alone?

A: She thought children should be seen and not herded!

Q: Why couldn't the cow leave the farm?

A: She was pasteurized!

Q: Why are cows made for dancing?

A: They're all born hoofers!

Q: Where does a cow stop to drink?

A: The Milky Way!

Q: Where do steers go to dance?

A: To the Meat Ball!

Q: Where do Russian cows come from?

A: Moscow!

Q: Where do milk shakes come from?

A: Nervous cows!

Q: Where do Danish cows come from?

A: Cowpenhagen.

Q: Where do cows like to ride on trains?

A: In the cow-boose.

Q: Where do cows like to live?

A: St. Moo-is.

Q: Where do baby cows eat?

A: To the calf-ateria!

Q: Where did the bull carry his stock-market report?

A: In his beef case!

Q: When is a farmer like a magician?

A: When he turns his cow into pasture.

Q: When a bull wants to listen to a cassette, what does he put on his head?

A: Steer phones!

Q: What's a cow's favorite musical note?

A: Beef-flat!

Q: What would you hear at a cow concert?

A: Moo-sic!

Q: What would you get if you crossed a cow with a rabbit?

A: Hare in your milk!

Q: What U.S. state has the most cows?

A: Moosouri!

Q: What two members of the cow family go everywhere with you?

A: Your calves!

Q: What South American dance do cows like to do?

A: The Rump-a!

Q: What sound do you hear when you drop a bomb on a cow?

A: Cowboom!

Q: What newspaper do cows read?

A: The Daily Moos.

Q: What magazine makes cows stampede to the newsstand?

A: Cows-mopolitan!

Q: What kind of cows do you find in Alaska?

A: Eski-moos!

Q: What is the most important use for cowhide?

A: To hold the cow together.

Q: What is the golden rule for cows?

A: Do unto udders as you would have udders do to you!

Q: What is the definition of moon?

A: The past tense of moo!

Q: What is the definition of derange?

A: De place where de cowboys ride!

Q: What is a cow's favorite lunchmeat?

A: Bullogna.

Q: What happens when a cow stops shaving?

A: It grows a moostache.

Q: What happens when the cows refuse to be milked?

A: Udder chaos!

Q: What hair style is a calves' favorite?

A: The cowlick!

Q: What happened to the lost cattle?

A: Nobody's herd.

Q: What gives milk and has a horn?

A: A milk tank!

Q: What goes oo ooo oooo?

A: A cow with no lips.

Q: What famous painting do cows love to look at?

A: The Mooona Lisa!

Q: What does a cow ride when his car is broken?

A: A COW-asaki MOO-torcycle!

Q: What does a cow like to do by a campfire?

A: Roast moosmallows!

Q: What do you get when you cross a cow with a kangaroo?

A: A kangamoo!

Q: What do you get if you cross Bossy with a vampire?

A: Dracowla!

Q: What do you get if you cross a steer and a chicken?

A: Roost beef!

Q: What do you get if you cross a longhorn with a knight?

A: Sir Loin!

Q: What do you get if you cross a cow, a French fry, and a sofa?

A: A cowch potato!

Q: What do you get if you cross a cow with a tension headache?

A: A bad mood!

Q: What do you get if you cross a cow with a spaniel, a poodle, and a rooster?

A: A cockerpoodlemoo!

Q: What do you get from pampered cows?

A: Spoiled milk!

Q: What do you get from an invisible cow?

A: Evaporated milk!

Q: What do you get from a short-legged cow?

A: Dragon milk!

Q: What do you get from a forgetful cow?

A: Milk of amnesia!

Q: What do you get from a cow on the North Pole?

A: Cold cream!

Q: What do you call it when one bull spies on another bull?

A: A steak-out!

Q: What do you call it when cows do battle in outer space?

A: Steer Wars.

Q: What do you call explosive cow vomit?

A: A cud missile!

Q: What do you call a herd of cows in a psychiatrist's office?

A: An encownter group.

Q: What do you call a cow who works for a gardener?

A: A lawn moo-er.

Q: What do you call a cow that's just had a baby?

A: De-calfinated!

Q: What do you call a cow that fell in a hole?

A: A hole-y cow!

Q: What do you call a tired cow?

A: Milked out!

Q: What do you call a cow that doesn't give milk?

A: A milk dud!

Q: What do you call a sleeping bull?

A: A bull-dozer.

Q: What do you call a group of cattle sent into orbit?

A: The first herd shot round the world!

Q: What do you call a cow with no front legs?

A: Lean Beef.

Q: What do you call a cow who argues with her husband?

A: A bullfighter!

Q: What do you call a cow on the barnyard floor?

A: Ground beef.

Q: What do you call a bull that's sent overseas by boat?

A: Shipped beef!

Q: What do you call a bull that runs into a threshing machine?

A: Hamburger!

Q: What do cows usually fly around in?

A: Helicowpters and bulloons.

Q: What do cows wear when they're vacationing in Hawaii?

A: Moo moos.

Q: What do cows sing at their friend's birthday parties?

A: Happy birthday to MOO, Happy Birthday to MOO.

Q: What do cows read at the breakfast table?

A: The moospaper!

Q: What do cows like to listen to?

A: Moo-sic!

Q: What do cows like to do at amusement parks?

A: Ride on the roller cowster.

Q: What do cows get when they do all their chores?

A: Mooney.

Q: What do cows get when they are sick?

A: Hay Fever.

Q: What do cows do when there introduced?

A: They give each other a milk shake!

Q: What do cows do for entertainment?

A: They go to the mooovies.

Q: What do cows call Frank Sinatra?

A: Old Moo Eyes!

Q: What did the moron say when he saw the milk cartons in the grass?

A: Hey! Look at the cows nest!

Q: What did the cow wear to the football game?

A: A jersey.

Q: What did the calf say to the silo?

A: Is my fodder in there?

Q: What did one dairy cow say to another?

A: Got milk?

Q: What country do cows love to visit?

A: Moo Zealand!

Q: What band is a cow favorite?

A: Moody Blues.

Q: What are cow's favorite party games?

A: MOO-sical chairs!

Q: What animals do you bring to bed?

A: Your calves.

Q: That tornado damage your cow barn any?

A: Not sure. Haven't found the darn thing yet!

Q: That bull you sold me is a lazy good-for-nothing!

A: I told you he was a bum steer!

Q: How to you know that cows will be in heaven?

A: It's a place of udder delight.

Q: How does a cow do math?

A: With a cowculator

Q: How do you make a milkshake?

A: Give a cow a pogo stick.

Q: How do bulls drive their cars?

A: They steer them!

Q: How did the farmer find his lost cow?

A: He tractor down.

Q: What do you call a cow that plays the guitar?

A: A moosician!

Q: How did the calf's final exam turn out?

A: Grade A!

Q: How did that bullfight come out?

A: Oh, it was a toss-up!

Q: How did cows feel when the branding iron was invented?

A: They were very impressed!

Q: Does running out of a burning barn make a cow unusual?

A: No, only medium rare!

Q: Did you hear about the snobby cow?

A: She thought she was a cutlet above the rest!

Q: Did you hear about the farmer who lost control of his tractor in the cow pasture?

A: No!

Q: Did he hurt the cows?

A: No, he just grazed them!

Q: I've just discovered a method for making wool out of milk!

A: But doesn't that make the cow feel a little sheepish?

Q: Is there big money in the cattle business?

A: So I've herd!

Q: In what state will you find the most cows?

A: Moo York!

Q: If you make a cow angry, how will she get even?

A: She'll cream you!

Q: If you crossed two cows with a flock of ducks, what would you get?

A: Milk and quackers!

Q: If you crossed a cow with Michael Jackson, what song would you get?

A: Beef it!

Q: If you crossed a cow with a goat, what would you get?

A: Half and half!

Q: What advice do cows give?

A: Turn the udder cheek and mooooove on!

MOO HOO JOKES

Q: What is a moo hoo for the bucket that goes at the back end of the cow?

A: A tail pail!

Q: What is a moo hoo for steak that came late?

A: Filet delay!

Q: What is a moo hoo for a sheepish steer?

A: A woolly bully!

Q: What is a moo hoo for a delightful ranch owner?

A: A charmer farmer!

Q: What is a moo hoo for a cow that fell into the thresher?

A: Ground round!

Q: What is a moo hoo for a cow fight?

A: A cattle battle!

Q: What's a moo hoo for the sound you hear when a cow spits?

A: A cud thud!

Q: What's a moo hoo for grazing school?

A: Grass class!

Q: What's a moo hoo for a young calf?

A: A new moo!

Q: What's a moo hoo for a tug-of-war between two longhorns?

A: A bull pull!

Q: What's a moo hoo for a stuffed steer?

A: A full bull!

Q: What's a moo hoo for a darling bull?

A: A dear steer!

Q: What's a moo hoo for a cow barn on a holiday?

A: A merry dairy!

Q: What's a moo hoo for a cattle dinner?

A: Cow chow!

Q: What's a moo hoo for a bunch of weirdo cattle?

A: A nerd herd!

COW MAZE

MAZE #1

MAZE #3

MAZE #4

COW MAZE SOLUTION

MAZE SOLUTIONS 1-4

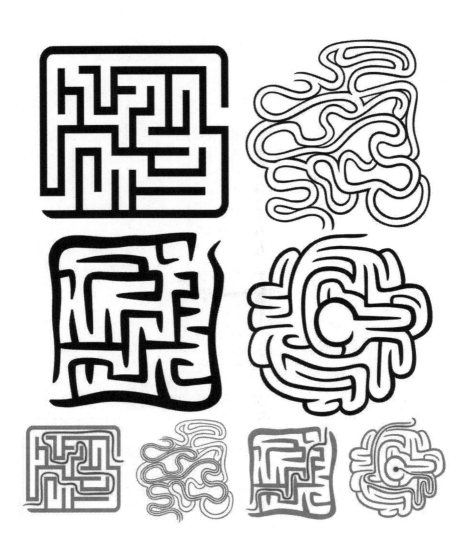

ABOUT THE AUTHOR

The Joke King, Johnny B. Laughing is a best-selling children's joke book author. He is a jokester at heart and enjoys a good laugh, pulling pranks on his friends, and telling funny and hilarious jokes!

For more funny joke books just search for JOHNNY B. LAUGHING on Amazon

-or-

Visit the website:
www.funny-jokes-online.weebly.com

Made in the USA
Las Vegas, NV
18 November 2022

59781680R00024